a MONSTER
WROTE ME a LETTER

Scholastic Canada Ltd.
604 King Street West, Toronto, Ontario M5V 1E1, Canada

Scholastic Inc.
557 Broadway, New York, NY 10012, USA

Scholastic Australia Pty Limited
PO Box 579, Gosford, NSW 2250, Australia

Scholastic New Zealand Limited
Private Bag 94407, Greenmount, Auckland, New Zealand

Scholastic Children's Books
Euston House, 24 Eversholt Street, London NW1 1DB, UK

Library and Archives Canada Cataloguing in Publication
Bland, Nick
A monster wrote me a letter / Nick Bland.
ISBN 978-0-439-93573-9
I. Title.
PZ7.B557Mo 2007   j823'.92   C2007-900151-3

ISBN - 10 0-439-93573-3

First published by Scholastic Australia in 2005
This edition published by Scholastic Canada Ltd. in 2007

6 5 4 3 2   Printed in Malaysia   07 08 09 10 11

a MONSTER WROTE ME a LETTER

NICK BLaND

Scholastic Canada Ltd.
Toronto New York London Auckland Sydney
Mexico City New Delhi Hong Kong Buenos Aires

The boy:

A monster wrote me a letter today.
He said he was coming to my house to play.

But what if he's scary and won't go away?
What if the monster decides to STAY?

But a scary monster wouldn't write—
He'd come and scare me late at night.
This monster chap is so polite,
He might not even scratch or bite.

I wonder if he's green or blue,
And if his teeth are poking through.
There's only one thing left to do:
I'll have to write a letter too.

The monster:

A little boy wrote me a letter today.
He thinks that I'm going to his house to play.
There's been a mistake, but what can I say?
He expects me there on Saturday!

The letter that he must have read
Was meant for Monster Cousin Fred,
Who lives there underneath the bed.
Now I must meet the boy instead!

I've never met a kid before.
I must remember not to roar,
Or hide behind his bedroom door.
He'd send me home at once, for sure!

The boy:

What on earth do monsters eat?
Sloppy slugs and rotten meat?

I'll have to find a monster treat,
Like codfish heads or lizard feet.

I'll put some prickles on the path,
And put piranhas in the bath.
I hope my voice is deep enough,
To grunt and groan instead of laugh.

The monster:

I'll have to wear a shirt that's white,
So I don't give the boy a fright.
I must remember not to bite,
Or creep around the house at night.

My fingernails will need a file.
I haven't bathed in quite a while.
I'll take a bath; I'll learn to smile;
I'll comb my hair in "people" style.

The boy:
I'll empty out the kitchen bin,
And make sure all the lights are dim.
I'll take the bowl the fish are in,
And fill it up with toads for him.

I'll put some cobwebs round the place,
And stick some green stuff on my face.
I'll bring my sister just in case
He needs another kid to chase.

Right on time, at half past four,
Came three soft knocks and nothing more.
I had one final practice roar,
And went to open up the door.

I must admit I've never seen
A monster look so nice and clean.
Apart from being short and green,
He didn't look the least bit mean.

He said, "Hi," and I said, "Boo!"
I asked him if his shoes were new.
He asked me how my prickles grew
So nice and thick—and pointy too.

I taught him how to catch a ball . . .

And use the phone to make a call.

He taught me how to creep and crawl . . .

And eat an apple, core and all.

Now he's moved in beneath my bed
To live there with his cousin Fred.
And when I'm scared, the monsters said
To wake them up and chat instead.

I'm not frightened anymore,
Of monsters crouched behind the door.
But one thing that I know for sure,
Those monsters really love to snore!